Just My Luck

Gwen Overland writing as,

Cunigunda Valentine

Copyright © 2018 Gwen Overland

All rights reserved.

ISBN: 8150906
ISBN-13: 978-0692142769

DEDICATION

This book is dedicated to all those who dream for a life of adventure, whether they have the courage to pursue it or not.

And a special dedication to my late maternal grandmother, whose name I have appropriated as my pen name for this series. I'll always love you, granny, for your humor, your strength, and your independent spirit.

Gwen Overland as Cunigunda Valentine

CONTENT USE

This is a work of fiction. Names, characters, places, and incidents are the product of the author's imagination or are used fictitiously. Any resemblance to actual persons, living or dead, business establishments, events, or locales is entirely coincidental.

All rights reserved. No part of this book may be reproduced, scanned, or distributed in any print or electronic form without the permission of the author.

Cover design by Rhian Awni.

Design and interior formatting by Erica Anderson

ACKNOWLEDGMENTS

To my trusted writer friends, Lisa H., Lisa C., Maisey, Megan, Vella, Cyndi, and Rusty—otherwise known as the Fellowship of the Bean—, thank you for taking the time to read my work and for providing valuable feedback.

A huge thanks to Rhian Awni for my extraordinary, playful cover art.

And as always, a huge thanks to my devoted family, who never seem to mind the hours I spend away from them doing what I love second to them.

And a special thanks to my late maternal grandmother, whose name I have appropriated for my pseudonym.

Chapter One

Kathryn Richards had no idea what hurt more – her aching back or her broken heart. She'd been driving sixteen hours straight since leaving Seattle. And still had another eight or nine hours to go before reaching L.A.

If only she had budgeted her money more wisely, then she might've had enough for a night's stay in a cheap motel. Which of course wasn't the most ideal of choices, but at least that would've gotten her out of this excuse-of-a-car and allowed her to stretch her legs. Take a quick shower. Or treat herself to a long nap. As it was, Kate barely had enough money for gas, and even less energy to make the long and arduous trek down the I-5 corridor.

Yet nothing compared to what she had gone through her last year of graduate studies at the University of Washington. What with classes, comprehensive exams and orals, and dealing with her dissertation committee (particularly one professor, Dr. Randall Carlyle by name), she was exhausted beyond anything she imagined she could endure. But it was all worth it, for at last she held her PhD diploma in Library Science in her hand and nothing or nobody was ever going to take that away from her.

Not even Randy.

The douche canoe.

"Oh, crap!" Kate blurted out as once again she found her eyes welling up with tears. When was she ever going to be done crying over this man who she thought loved her as much as she loved him?

Soon, her mind kept assuring her. But her heart kept

repeating not yet.

Still the tears came whenever she thought about how stupid she had been to get herself romantically mixed up with the one professor who served as her dissertation chair. True, Randy—that is, Dr. Carlyle—had been super kind, respectful and irresistibly handsome. Unfortunately, however, and unbeknownst to her, he also had been married.

"Idiot! Idiot! Idiot!" Kate chanted as she pounded on the steering wheel of her 1967 Volkswagen Convertible Bug, no longer directing her anger at Mr. Sexy Ass Hat, but solely at herself. "For an overly educated woman, Dr. Richards, you're sure a dunce!" she scolded as she turned off the freeway to gas up at the first station she spotted.

For the umpteenth time Kate found herself standing in an ice cold, stinky public bathroom splashing water on her swollen face and reapplying what little makeup she had brought with her for the trip. As she gazed into the mirror, Kate noted with each pit stop her face was becoming less puffy and her crying less frequent.

"Criminy!" she said out loud. "By the time I get to LA I may actually be over that turd!"

Kate then put on her best fake smile as she pointed at her reflection. "It's show time!" she pronounced to no one other than herself. And then shoved her things back into her oversized tote—the Jimmy Choo knock off she bought at Wal-Mart for one sixteenth of the going price. And made a bee-line for the cashier, where she not only paid for her gas, but a few *necessary* snacks to tide her over.

A box of Junior Mints.

A can of Diet Coke.

And a two-pill packet of Aleve.

After checking all four tires to make sure they still held enough air to complete her trip, Kate crawled back behind the wheel of the only vehicle she had ever owned and aimed the front grill toward her final destination. She had been lucky to have been given the car by Grammy Lou, one of the few friends she made so far in her short life.

Louise Pederson had been Kate's case worker all the years she lived in foster care. And unlike the many foster moms Kate had been subjected to, Grammy Lou truly cared about Kate. And offered her the kind of stability and encouragement she needed as a young girl and teen.

But even Grammy Lou was now gone, having passed away several years earlier from a sudden heart attack, leaving Kate with many treasured memories as well as an ancient car with low mileage.

Kate was also fortunate that the first job since graduation waited for her at the prestigious University of California, Los Angeles. Assistant Research Librarian for the main library on campus was nothing to sneeze at. And after all the hoopla between her and her dissertation chair, Kate knew how lucky she was to have gotten out of Seattle with her degree, let alone a job offer!

And a chance to start over.

Again.

In fact, Kate was a bona fide expert at the starting over game. From the time she left the orphanage in Tacoma as a young girl of seven, to the many foster families she was shifted to and from over the next ten years, Kate had grown accustomed to new beginnings and at the same time more wary of them. As far as she was concerned, starting over was over rated.

By far.

For each move seemed more like a merry-go-round of repeated experiences rather than a betterment of her circumstances. And even now, though Kate had put a great deal of faith into this next adventure, something in the back of her mind warned her to be careful. After all, given her experience things seldom turned out the way she expected.

To pass the time Kate had no other recourse but to sing every song she could remember beyond the first two lines. This she did at the top of her lungs with the window rolled down so as to allow the cool early morning air to help her stay awake.

After several attempts to get through the few songs she thought she remembered, Kate finally settled on *The Wabash Cannonball*, a tune which took her back to her childhood. Whenever Grammy Lou took Kate out for an afternoon away from her foster situation, the two of them sang along to Lou's favorite Loretta Lynn cassette tape which she played over and over again ad nauseum. But those days were long gone, as were the Volkswagen's radio and tape player.

From the great Atlantic ocean

to the wide Pacific shore...

The sunrise over the grapevine was extraordinary. Purples, peaches, periwinkle blues and baby bottom pinks vividly danced across the sky as Kate weaved through the hills before making her descent into LA County proper.

She had more than enough time to take in all the sights as the VW could only negotiate the hilly incline at 35 miles an hour. And that was with her foot jammed on the gas pedal all the way down to the floorboard. Luckily, Kate wheedled her car in between two slow-moving trucks, and like a caravan of sated camels, together the three vehicles trudged across the Tehachapi mountain range.

From the queen of flowing mountain

to the south bell by the shore...

With one eye on the truck in front of her and the other on the temperature gauge, in slow motion Kate rehashed the events surrounding her situation one nerve-wracking detail at a time. Sleep deprived and high from way too much sugar and caffeine, her mind pinged from one imagined outcome to the next. Everything was now impingent upon her new job. Her new California life.

It wasn't uncommon for Kate's mind to wander into an elaborate fantasy world whenever she became nervous about her future. Especially during those times in her childhood when things in reality didn't always look as if they were going in her favor.

True, she had her degree and a new job waiting for her, but she also had no money, no place to live, and not one friend in the world to turn to. She was utterly, inextricably, and frightfully alone.

She's mighty tall and handsome and known quite well by all

She's the combination on the Wabash Cannonball!

Curious as to her speed, Kate glanced down at the dashboard and noticed once again the needle on the gas gauge read close to empty.

"Oh, crap!"

She had been so transfixed by the horror flick playing in her mind, she not only forgot about her fuel, but nearly missed the 405 cut off—the freeway interchange which would take her through one last valley before she made the UCLA/Sunset Boulevard exit.

All she could do now was pray her 1967 Volkswagen Convertible had enough fumes to coast into the campus parking lot. It wouldn't be a good thing for her to be late for the first day of work. Or even worse, a no-show.

As a last ditch gas saving technique, Kate leaned into the steering wheel as if the weight of her body would somehow propel her car forward. She wasn't sure many red lights she would have to run or how many stop signs she would have to roll through, but arrive at her destination she would. Even if she had to push her fuel-deprived car all the way.

At least she knew where the visitor lot was located given her internet research expertise.

I mean, I've a PhD in Library Science, for heaven's sake! Kate smirked at the thought. She was obviously under qualified for the job she had been hired for, yet over qualified in nearly every other area of her life. She was well read, had been in love, could change the oil and any one of a dozen flat tires on an economy size car. And could expertly cook all things Italian. She even spoke fluent French and German. But still she felt behind the eight ball.

Oh well, once a foster kid, always a foster kid.

The Bug rolled into the parking lot slightly before 6 a.m. Kate didn't have to show up for work until nine, so she talked herself into closing her eyes for a short nap before freshening up to start her day. Perhaps it was the tension of the last few hours or the months of getting little or no sleep, but before she counted to three, Kate was out.

Completely and thoroughly zonked.

Her hands still fisted the steering wheel. But her head was thrown back, her mouth wide open, and the most unladylike sounds emptied out her mouth. Along with a sizeable amount of drool. Kate had been told she snored like a sailor. But because she was always asleep at the time of said snoring, she wasn't aware of the ferocity with which she did so. She remembered once sawing logs so loudly she woke herself up, but she merely chalked it up to a once in a lifetime experience. And that was all there was to it. For now, however, the months of hard work and a long ass drive had caught up to her and she surrendered to her body's demand for sleep.

***

Every day for the last forty years Professor Marcel Ricardou strode briskly from his undersized but cozy home in Westwood to his faculty office on campus. His tenure as a full professor in the French department was well noted by many of the faculty, staff and students working at or attending UCLA.

For one thing, he always wore a beige trench coat, a dark brown beret, and one of the two rumpled suits he still owned from purchasing them the first years of teaching. On top of that, he always waxed his mustache and smoked the dark black Galois cigarettes which his country of origin was noted for.

His leather valise, stuffed with papers, appeared as if a miniature bomb had gone off on the inside causing crumpled papers to hang out all along its edges. His face was fixed with a slight smile, and if anyone got close enough, they could hear him humming any one of the many popular French songs of his youth. He was an eccentric—a character out of a novel.

He was also known for his sweet demeanor and deep care for his students. In spite of the fact he was now fully retired, Doctor Ricardou never missed a day of showing up to his office. Although he no longer found himself in the classroom, he had a true passion for research. Some habits are too hard to break.

Professor Ricardou loved his early morning and late afternoon treks from his home to his office and back for it gave him a chance to gather his thoughts and reformulate his to-do list for the day at hand. Rarely was he ever distracted except for once in a while when odd sights, sounds or odors forced him out of his head and into the present. And this morning was simply one of those occasions.

Hooooonnnnnkkkkk! Hooooonnnnnkkkkk!

He stopped and searched for where the sound was coming from.

Hooooonnnnnkkkkk! Hooooonnnnnkkkkk!

Not a single car or truck sped past on the closest street to him

Hooooonnnnnkkkkk! Hooooonnnnnkkkkk!

That meant the horn must be from a parked vehicle, he reasoned.

Hooooonnnnnkkkkk! Hooooonnnnnkkkkk!

Then out of the corner of his eye he saw what appeared to be like an old abandoned junkyard relic. Except for the slumped over body of a young woman in the driver's seat, her forehead leaning against the car's steering wheel.

"*Mon Dieu!* I hope to God she isn't dead!"

Hooooonnnnnkkkkk! Hooooonnnnnkkkkk!

Quickly the old professor glanced around him to see if anyone else could come to the woman's aid, but there wasn't a single soul in sight.

"*Merde!*"

Hooooonnnnnkkkkk! Hooooonnnnnkkkkk!

"*Alors,* what to do? I can't simply leave her here." The professor hemmed and hawed for a few more seconds before mustering his courage.

Hooooonnnnnkkkkk! Hooooonnnnnkkkkk!

Doctor Ricardou cautiously peeked through the driver's side window to determine if he could see any gashes or wounds about the woman's body.

"*Rien.* Nothing."

Whenever Marcel Ricardou needed the appropriate boldness to approach a tenuous situation, he usually found it by talking out loud to himself. He wasn't clear as to why that simple act appeared to work, but it always did.

Hooooonnnnnkkkkk! Hooooonnnnnkkkkk!

Finally Professor Ricardou did the only thing he could think of next. He bravely knocked on the woman's window.

"Hallo? Mademoiselle? Are you in need of assistance, *s'il vous plaît?*"

Hooooonnnnnkkkkk! Hooooonnnnnkkkkk!

Kate wasn't sure if what she heard was real or a dream. For she was so deep into dreamland, she could hardly budge herself awake. The pounding sound had to be the headache she felt beginning right behind the ridge of her eyebrows.

"Huh?' she softly groaned.

Hooooonnnnnkkkkk! Hooooonnnnnkkkkk!

The woman in front of Marcel Ricardou began to stir. "Mademoiselle, if you can hear me, please let me know if you're okay or not."

He rapped on the window until he thought his knuckles would bleed.

"In either case I'm here to assist you."

Hooooonnnnnkkkkk! Hon . . .

As soon as Kate heard a man's voice, her eyes popped open wide, the tension in her body forcing her to sit straight up in her seat. For a brief second she forgot where she was and how she had gotten there.

"What the . . .?" She then turned her head and saw through her dirty side window the figure of an odd looking gentleman smiling back at her.

Relieved to no longer have to listen to the incessant barrage of the horn, Marcel beamed with relief. And joy, for not only was the young woman all right, but she was quite stunning in a peculiar, almost comic way.

Her auburn hair was mussed and her glasses askew. Plus, the imprint of the steering wheel evidenced itself in the several indentations of her forehead and cheeks. And if he wasn't mistaken, the girl had what looked like a medley of chocolate and beef jerky hanging off the sides of her mouth. Yet, in spite of her disarray, the young woman was actually rather cute, pretty in fact, in a sweet but whacky Lucille Ball kind of way.

"Mademoiselle, permit me to introduce myself. I'm Professor Emeritus Marcel Ricardou. I heard your car horn and wondered if you in some way needed my help. But I see now you were merely asleep—at the wheel, so to speak. Please, open the door so I may ascertain your injuries!"

Kate took one look at the apparition before her and screamed at the top of her lungs.

"HELP!"

Chapter Two

Kate had heard stories about the crazies who lived in Los Angeles, but she never imagined the first person she would meet upon her arrival would be such a person.

"Mademoiselle, I assure you. I mean you no harm. As I said, I'm Professor Marcel Ricardou of the Foreign Language Department here at UCLA. I heard your car horn and saw what appeared to be unconsciousness on your part or at the very least serious distress. Please, let me give my card."

The frazzled professor searched the pockets of his overcoat but found them to be empty save a cigarette lighter and a few coins. Finally he reached inside his overcoat and took out a tiny jeweled box about the size of a toothpick holder, opened it, selected the top card and presented it at Kate's tightly closed window.

Kate squinted through the glass trying to read the miniscule print. The closer her nose and mouth got to the window, however, the more steamed up the inside of her car became. She rubbed a small opening into the moist film with her fist. Peering through the hole, Kate still couldn't read the undersized print. It was then she realized she was wearing her driving glasses and not her readers, which unfortunately were packed in one of her suitcases in the back of the Bug.

"Now look, Mister. I'm going to roll my window down a crack, room enough for you to push your card through the slot. Okay?"

"*Bien sûr*, Mademoiselle, but of course, I understand."

The professor smiled warmly as he watched the

young woman roll her window down no more than a quarter of an inch—an act of insurmountable courage on her part. As soon as Kate took and the card and read it as best she could, she blushed a deep crimson.

Hiccup!

And then hiccupped.

Horrified she could've mistaken the professor for a serial killer, Kate glimpsed sheepishly into the eyes of her rescuer.

"Professor Ricardou, I apologize for not believing who you said you were. My name's Kathryn Richards and I'm the new assistant librarian at the campus research library. Today's my first day of work, but because I drove here straight through from Seattle, I'm afraid I dozed off without realizing it. Please, forgive me for being so rude."

Kate did her best to pry herself out of her car. But as soon as she stood in front of the meticulously groomed professor, she blushed a second time. Her silk blouse and chino pants were a landscape of wrinkles.

Hiccup!

Of course, she hiccupped again.

Ah-choo!

Followed by a sneeze.

Her nerves often had this odd way of presenting themselves.

Marcel snatched the beret off his head and ran a hand over the top of his bald pate. "The fault is mine, Mademoiselle Richards. Sometimes I presume too much. At least, this is what my wife often says."

He then grinned and winked at Kate's startled expression. "In any case, welcome to our beautiful campus."

Kate couldn't help but notice the kindness behind the eyes of the sweet yet shy professor. "Thank you, Professor

. . ."

—she glared down at the business card she held in her hand—"Professor Marcel Ricardou." She answered smiling back. "You wouldn't happen to know the time would you?"

"*Alors,* I'm afraid I don't have the exact time, but I believe it's close to 7:30. What time do you need to be at work?"

"I'm supposed to meet Dr. Woodman at her office in the research library at 9:45."

"Ah, then you have time to share a *petit dejeuner* with me, *n'est pas?*"

"Uh . . ."

Kate wasn't as up with her French as she was her Italian.

"Please, Mademoiselle Richards," he continued, "allow me to treat you to breakfast at the faculty lounge.

There we can have a short visit and you may refresh yourself should you need." The professor, glancing at Kate's creased clothing and unkempt hair, did his best not to let on how discombobulated his new friend appeared. He was far too gracious to even think of doing so.

But Kate was no fool. She knew she looked like something the dog dragged in, which simply wasn't going to work on this her first day at the new job. For pity's sake, she didn't even have on a pair of shoes—just her lucky U of Dub Huskies knee high socks complete with little puppy faces and miniature bones! Even they seemed to be a bit worse for wear. Twisted around her ankles with a hole in the big toe of one and a sizeable rip in the grease stained heel of the other.

"Ahhh!" she sighed. "I think I had best take you up on your lovely offer, Professor Ricardou! I must look like a crazy woman!"

"No, no, no, Mademoiselles! You look . . . huh . . . refreshed! Yes, that's it—refreshed! And please, call me Marcel."

Kate started to giggle. *What a nice guy!* She thought to herself. "And you in turn must call me Kate. All my very best friends do!"

While Kate gathered her things from the car, Professor Ricardou placed an additional business card under the windshield wiper of her car. "That's to make sure your car will not be towed. The campus police are quite serious here on campus. And a bit ticket happy, if you know what I mean." The Frenchman wiggled his eyebrows as he grinned.

As a recent college student herself, Kate was no stranger to the moniker "rent a cop" as her fellow students called the campus police. She personally had never had to call upon their services, and she wasn't about to do so today. Besides, she had absolutely no money to spare for a parking ticket, or worse—the cost of having her car impounded.

"I know exactly what you mean! And thank you for this. I know I don't exactly look all that promising as a new UCLA employee." Kate agreed as she unrolled and latched the convertible's rag top in place and then followed her new-found friend toward their destination.

***

Once in the building Kate excused herself and headed toward the women's restroom. One look in the mirror and she blanched. There on her chocolate smudged chin sat not only evidence of her Junior Mint binge, but something which suspiciously gave the impression of dried drool.

"Piss! Shit! Crap! Douche Bag!" she blurted out in front of a woman emerging from a nearby stall. Dressed in a light grey wool suit and looking fifty times more put together than Kate, the woman lifted her right eyebrow in disapproval.

"Sorry! I didn't know anyone else was in here."

Shut up, Kate. You're only making things worse.

But try as she may, Kate couldn't keep quiet.

"You see, I slept in my car last night. Well, actually early this morning. I suppose it could still be considered last night. Anyway, I didn't realize until now most of my supper ended up on my chin."

Oh damn, damn, triple damn!

"And some other stuff."

Shut up already!

The woman eyed Kate as if she were an escapee from some nearby mental health institution.

"I don't believe I've seen you around before," the woman said in a clipped tone. "If you don't mind me asking dear, are you an employee here on campus? After all, this is the *faculty* lounge."

Kate heard the snooty emphasis the woman placed on the word *faculty* and wanted to smack her. But she refused to let the woman get to her. And so calmly smiled.

"Not yet, I mean yes. Actually, yes. That is to say, I will be in close to an hour from now."

The woman stared at Kate in the mirror as she washed her hands. "Well, good luck dear. You're obviously going to need it!" She continued to wipe her well manicured hands on the provided paper towel as she sped out of the restroom.

Kate returned her gaze to the mirror. "You certainly handled that well," she sarcastically spit out as she continued to wash her face. "Idiot!"

Kate finished her grooming ritual at the sink with a quick one-two. Applied new makeup, and combed her hair into a twist at the back of her head. The "do" wasn't all that flattering, but she was after all merely a college librarian and not a Playboy bunny.

Although that certainly would be interesting!

So much for her wandering mind! Time to get back to the delightful Monsieur Ricardou and his peculiarly thin moustache.

Kate glanced both ways before leaving the safety of the Ladies Lounge. She certainly didn't want to run into the same persnickety woman if she could avoid it. And if she did, Kate would have no problem letting her know a thing or two.

Just because I look a bit tired and wrinkled doesn't give anyone including that old biddy permission be so rude.

Hiccup!

"So there!"

Ah-choo!

Kate hustled back to her seat at the professor's table where he stood waiting her arrival.

"Ah, Mademoiselle Kathryn, you look, how do you say, refreshed?"

"Oui! I mean, yes, I do. That is, I am. *Refreshed.*"

As a matter of fact, Kate appeared many times better than she did merely moments ago. Amazing what a change of clothes and a tube of lipstick could do for a girl!

The two sat at a table for two tucked away in the corner of the dining area. The room itself was more functional than fancy. In front of her sat a durable china place setting featuring the university emblem on the dinner plate, a delicate coffee cup and saucer to match, and silverware with the prongs of the fork bent in several different directions. All this was held up by a clean white tablecloth which had seen better days.

"I took the opportunity to order for the two of us

while you were being refreshed. I hope you don't mind."

"Of course not. That was very kind of you." Kate knew she had been in the ladies room longer than she had hoped to be. But it takes more than a couple minutes to straighten out a full day's wrinkles and candy smudges.

Kate instinctively leaned in to sniff the tiny flower separating her from her dining companion. But before she inhaled, Kate immediately saw it was artificial, its plastic stem smashed inside the bottom of its plastic vase. She reached to pick it up for a closer look, her curiosity getting the better of her.

"Is there something the matter, Mademoiselle?" The professor asked, careful not to betray the smile forming behind his concern.

Mon Dieu, but this woman has an inquisitive soul!

"Huh?"

"The flower?" he coaxed.

"Oh, yes. The flower. I mean, no. No, there's nothing the matter. It's just that . . ."

"It's fake. *Artificiale!*"

That sexy baritone voice couldn't possibly belong to Professor Ricardou. Could it?

Kate peeked up to where the voice had come from and immediately flushed. There, standing before her, was possibly the most handsome man she had ever met in her life. And she had met some good lookers in her past.

"Ah, Roberto!" exclaimed the old professor. "And how are you this morning, *amico mio?*"

"Molto bene, grazie. And I can see you are not doing so badly yourself." The man smiled, raised his right eyebrow, and Kate thought for sure she was going to pass out.

Quickly Marcel Ricardou stood to his feet. "You're referring to my new friend, no doubt. Mademoiselle

Kathryn, may I introduce you to my esteemed colleague, Roberto Cassinelli, chair of the Italian department. Roberto, Kathryn Richards, our new research librarian."

"Enchantez, Mademoiselle Katerina. Welcome to our beautiful campus!" He took her hand in his and bent over to kiss it. When he glanced back up, Kate could see his eyes were the same sexy chocolate brown as her freshly poured coffee.

"Grazie, Signore!" she squeaked and immediately hiccupped

The old professor took his seat. "Kathryn arrived early this morning after driving straight through from her home in Seattle. I couldn't help but rescue her from a morning with no breakfast. So, here we are. Would you care to join us?"

Kate hoped he would, at the same time she hoped he wouldn't.

"Molto grazie, Marcel. I would indeed!" The handsome Italian pulled a chair from a nearby empty table over to sit between Kathryn and his old friend.

Damn! Why does he have to be so good-looking?!

Kate watched as the Joe Manganiello look-alike leaned back in his chair, his arm draped over the back, exposing his long athletic thighs which pulled at the fabric of his pants.

"Roberto's the faculty advisor of the French Film Club here on campus." Marcel was doing his best to introduce Kate to the possible perks of her new job.

Roberto smiled at the mention of his name. "Do you enjoy the cinema, Signorina?"

"Uh . . ."

I would certainly enjoy you!

Ah-choo!

Well this is just great!

"Salute!" The two men answered in unison.

"I ... uh ..."

The more Kate thought about it, the more she realized she hadn't been to a movie since Grammy Lou took her to see *The Lion King* twenty years ago.

*(Nants ingonyama bagithi Baba
Sithi uhm ingonyama)*

Roberto placed his hand gently on her shoulder. "It is all right to admit you do not care for the cinema, Signorina, if that is indeed how you feel." Instantly she felt the heat from his body flood up her arm and into her lady parts.

Hiccup!

"It's not that. I simply haven't been able to see many movies of late due to graduate school and all. 'No time no money!'" she said with a half-hearted giggle.

"Then we must change that!" said Professor Ricardou enthusiastically. "Isn't that so, Robert?"

"*Sì, certo*! Of course! I will personally make sure you come as my guest."

Ah-choo!

"Salute!"

Professor Ricardou handed Kate his last clean handkerchief. "Are you feeling all right, Mademoiselle? I've noticed since Roberto arrived you sneeze quite frequently."

"Perhaps she is allergic to me! Ha!!" Roberto teased to put Kate at ease.

Allergic to this magnificent specimen of unspoiled masculinity? Never!

Marcel scrutinized his new found friend's face in an attempt to measure her apparent uncomfortability but was surprised to see her instead giggling at Roberto's every word. *Mon Dieu! He has bewitched yet another unsuspecting victim!*

"If I'm allergic to anything, it's the fragrant eucalyptus trees here on your beautiful campus." Kate quickly countered. "They give off an aroma I never experienced having grown up in the Pacific Northwest. There the pine and cedar trees can give me fits for months!" *Good cover, Kate.*

Ever since she was a child Kate had exhibited her nervousness in the most inappropriate ways. And always with peculiar variations of hiccupping or sneezing fits. And sometimes if she were in abject crisis, flatulence would rear its ugly head.

Marcel instantly saw through Kate's ruse but was polite enough not to call her on it. "I too had the same reaction when I moved here years ago. We've no eucalyptus trees in Paris. So how was I to know?"

"Indeed!" remarked Roberto. "The aroma reminds me of my childhood. Many of these trees surround Roma. *Bellisimi alberi!*"

Before Kate could respond the three were interrupted by the arrival of their food. And just in time as her growling stomach threatened to take over the conversation.

"My goodness!" exclaimed Kate. "This looks absolutely delicious!"

Before her the waiters arranged plates of scrambled eggs, bacon, pork sausage links, hash browns and everything else imaginable to compliment the bountiful array of breakfast items.

"Ah, you have outdone yourself again, Marcel!" teased Roberto as he dug into a stack of blueberry pancakes.

Kate stared at Roberto behind her triple shot latte as he savored his breakfast, his eyes closed and mouth in a half smile.

Good Jesus, he was dreamy! And for the first time in months Kate found she was losing her appetite for food in direct proportion to what she was gaining in deep appreciation for the Italian mystique.

Chapter Three

Time flew by faster than Kate had hoped. To be in the company of such exemplary gentlemen as Professors Marcel Ricardou and Roberto Cassinelli was heaven personified, for one was as sweet as the other was hot. But now it was finally time for her to start her first day at her new job and she didn't want to be late.

"Thank you so much for the lovely breakfast, Marcel," she said as she stood. Both men immediately took to their feet.

Ah, the Europeans!

The little Frenchman quickly took his clothe napkin in hand and daubed his moustache before taking Kate's in his other. "It was my profound pleasure, mademoiselle. We shall do it again soon, yes?" He gazed up at her with a mischievous twinkle in his eyes before kissing the back of said hand.

"Oh!" squeaked a startled Kate.

That was unexpected!

"Yes, that would be very nice. Indeed. Um . . ."

Not to be outdone, Roberto placed his huge warm hand on the back of her elbow and gently maneuvered her to face him. "Signorina, may I have the honor of escorting you to your destination? I guarantee I will get you there on time and in one piece." He then wiggled his perfectly manicured eyebrows as if to suggest his real intention was to do anything but.

Not at all sure as to how to respond, Kate answered the only way she could.

Ah-choo.

Followed by . . .

Hiccup.

Professor Ricardou, unable to hide his disapproval, scowled at his colleague. "Now, Roberto, no need to impose yourself upon the mademoiselle. I'm sure she's more than capable of finding the library on her own. Is that not so, Kate?"

"Eh . . ."

The truth of it was: she was totally, completely and entirely able to make her way to the research library. She had memorized the building's location from her internet search two nights prior. But it was also true that she could think of nothing in this moment more pleasant than having this deliciously sexy Italian impose himself all over her body, starting with her mouth and working his way down the front of her . . .

Ah-choo.

"Sorry. I still seem to be fighting some kind of allergic reaction."

God, I hate my life.

"Might I suggest we *both* accompany our newfound friend to the library?" suggested the elderly professor. "That way Ms Kate will benefit from the brilliance of two overly intelligent and frightfully handsome men at the same time."

"Ah, Marcel! You always come up with the cleverest of propositions. What do you say, Signorina Kathryn?" Roberto asked and then grinned back in what came across as something bordering on a grimace.

Try as she may, Kate couldn't tell if the men were competing for her attention or playing games with one another, but something was oddly peculiar about both of their behaviors.

Yet, not seeing any harm in having either one of

them, or the two of them together for that matter, stroll with her across campus, she agreed to have them tag along as she mentally prepared for her first day.

As soon as the three left the faculty lounge, Roberto took Kate's arm and placed it through his own. Not to be outdone, Marcel offered to carry her overstuffed tote so as to lighten her load.

"So tell me, Signorina Kathryn," drooled Roberto, "are you at all interested in joining me this evening at our weekly French Club meeting? We will be viewing a classic. Perhaps you have already seen it. *Last Year at Marienbad?*"

Kate couldn't believe her ears. This gorgeous hunk of Italian maleness had just asked her out on a date. Well, not exactly a date. But still . . .

"Well, if I've seen it before, I certainly don't remember . . ."

"*Mon Dieu*, Roberto!" Marcel exclaimed passionately.

"You aren't going to show that boring excuse for cinematic expertise again so soon, are you? We want Kate to join our club, not run away the first fifteen minutes of her visit?"

Without a second's worth of warning Roberto abruptly stopped where he stood, forcing Kate to nearly trip over both his feet and her own.

"What are you insinuating, Marcel?" he said as he turned to face his arrogant friend.

"I'm not insinuating anything. I'm merely speaking the truth. That film's nothing more than an overrated example of philosophical drivel!" Marcel answered as he poked Roberto in the chest.

"A masterpiece!" Roberto said as he shook his finger in Marcel's face.

"Pretentious twaddle!"

"A work of genius!"

"Incomprehensible mumbo jumbo!"

"A magnum opus!"

"Infantile poppy-cock!"

"*Cahiers du cinema* declared it to be a work of extreme importance, from the setting to the actor portrayals."

"Ha! An immense exaggeration!! You're only saying that because you fashion yourself to be a reincarnation of Giorgio Albertazzi, possibly the most boring actor on the face of the planet!"

"What do you know, you opinionated excuse for a French critic?!

Kate tried without success to interrupt the two professors, but they were too far into their sparring session to notice her tip-toeing away. She had two minutes left to accomplish at least four minutes worth of brisk walking.

Her new boss, Dr. Marian Woodman, had last week on the phone sounded as if she were all business. Normally

Kate would hardly give this fact the time of day, but needing the job as desperately as she did and not wanting to make a poor impression, she took off at a vigorous jog.

She was beginning to feel pretty good about her speed and athleticism until she reached the building itself and saw the several flights of stairs leading up to the front doors. She immediately stopped, took in two enormous gulps of air, put her head down, and on the count of three, raced up the stairs two at a time. As she ran past the checkout area, Kate blurted out "Dr. Woodman?" And a student worker pointed to the back of the first floor stacks.

Kate heard the campus chimes toll the hour, giving her the fuel she needed to whisk her way into the glass enclosed office which bore Dr. Woodman's full name and title 'Head Librarian' on the door. Behind the only desk visible sat a woman with her back facing Kate, busy filing papers into a two drawer cabinet, her keys hanging from the lock.

Not wanting to startle the poor creature, Kate cleared her throat and then addressed her by name. "Good Morning, Dr. Woodman?"

Without looking up the woman spun around in her chair to face Kate head on. "You're late!"

Ah shit, it's her! "Ah shit, it's you! I mean, shoot. I mean, sorry. I didn't mean to be late but I was delayed . . . um . . ."

Ah-choo!

Kate couldn't believe her eyes. There in front of her sat the same snotty woman who had addressed her in the faculty lounge restroom. *Please, please, please, don't let this be Dr. Woodman.*

"I wondered when I saw you earlier if you were the same Kathryn Richards whom I had hired for the position here, but I put the notion out of my mind as soon as I thought it. 'Certainly,' I said, 'she can't be the same woman I hired.' But apparently I was wrong."

Oh shoot, oh shoot, oh shoot! Hiccup!

"Sorry. I had to drive straight through from Seattle to Los—"

"Miss Richards!" Dr. Woodman interrupted as she stood. "I'm not a woman overly fond of excuses so please keep whatever you have to say to yourself."

Kate gazed down at the floor.

"Yes ma'am."

And fought an anxiety-ridden urge to stick her thumb in her mouth. The tail of Kate's blouse hung on the outside of her skirt, while a healthy bead of sweat stood at attention on her upper lip. For a brief moment she flashed back to her unpleasant childhood years in foster care. If only Grammy Lou were here to stand up for her!

Dr. Woodman slowly skulked her way toward Kate,

paused threateningly, then turned to seat her wrinkle-free fanny on the edge of her way too clean desk. Kate tried not to flinch, but all her energy was being siphoned toward not sneezing or hiccupping. The woman was a good foot shorter, but Kate swore Dr. Woodman could take her down in one swift kick.

"Look, Kathryn," the beast folded her arms defiantly. "I'm prepared to overlook your tardiness this one day, since it's your first and all. But after this, I expect you to be here at least fifteen minutes before the beginning of your shift, looking presentable and ready for a day's work. Do you think you can manage that?"

If I didn't need this job as badly as I do.... Kate lifted her head and stared eye to eye with the woman. "Yes, ma'am, you can count on me to do my job."

"Good! Now, I'm going to start you in our binding department. You might as well get acquainted with this library system from the torn and missing pages on up."

It was true. Kate was willing to do whatever it took to keep her position, but book repair? She quickly went through a mental check list of what had been listed in the job description and book repair wasn't included. If it had been, she more than likely wouldn't have applied since she didn't have the foggiest as to how to transform a damaged book into something beautiful and usable once again.

She was a researcher, and a good one at that. Yet, Kate knew when she was beaten, so she merely smiled (rather disingenuously) and reluctantly nodded her head in acceptance to Dr. Woodman's offer.

"Thank you, Dr. Woodman. I agree. Sometimes it's best to begin in the basement and work one's way up."

"That may be true. But in your case, binding's on the top floor. You'll need the natural light to see what you're doing. It's imperative the quality standards set by this university and the entire California university system are met. Do you think you can do that?"

Dr. Woodman stood, crossed the room, and retrieved the keys hanging from the coat bracket on the wall next to her suit coat. It took everything Kate had not to make faces silently mimicking the woman behind her back. Instead she took in a deep breath to quiet her deep hurt and frustration.

"Absolutely, Dr. Woodman. I'm always eager to learn new things." *Like how to choke you from behind and get away with murder . . .*

"Good," said her boss without looking at her. "Follow me and I'll show you where you'll be spending the next few months."

Months? Wha-?

"Yes, Ma'am."

Sodden cow! Millicent frantically trotted behind the

quick-footed Marian Woodman toward the service elevator.

"Everything you'll need is in the cabinets next to your work desk. The materials should all be self explanatory, but should you need help, please don't call me."

As soon as they stepped inside the elevator, Dr. Woodman hit several buttons on the panel, causing the doors to close. "Rather, view one of the many instruction videos on YouTube. Then if you still have questions, perhaps it will behoove us both if we each reevaluate your position here at UCLA."

Kate gasped at the same time the elevator jerked to a stop. The doors had barely opened before Dr. Woodman had somehow squeezed into the spacious empty room lit only by the natural light coming in through the many bare windows. As Dr. Woodman marched across the expanse, dust plumes rose into the air, giving the space an eerie fog-like atmosphere. Kate struggled to breathe as she jogged to keep up with her.

"Ah-choo! Excuse me, Dr. Woodman, but does anyone else work on this floor? Ah-choo!"

"Actually, it's been some time since we've had a full time employee relegated to binding, which is why we need someone to take over these duties before our backlog becomes too overburdened. As you can see, we've enough books and periodicals here to keep a person busy for months, if not years." Dr. Woodman grinned at her maliciously. At least that's the way it appeared to Kate.

"Yes, I . . . uh . . . I can see that. But Dr. Woodman, when I spoke to you on the phone last month about this position, you didn't mention book binding as part of my duties . . ."

"Oh, but I'm sure I did, Kathryn. You simply don't remember."

When the two women arrived at what seemed like the

only desk on the entire floor, Dr. Woodman unlocked the front desk drawer and handed Kate a set of keys. "These are yours, Kathryn, and will open every cabinet and drawer on this floor. And don't be thrown off by the worn out look of this phone." She pointed to something which seemed like a prop from the old *I Love Lucy* television show of the 1960s. "It will dial both on and off campus numbers but not long distance."

Kate stared down at the more than fifty keys in her hands.

"For now, why don't you seat yourself in this nice big desk chair—", she took Kate by the shoulders and plopped her down on the bare wooden pad of the chair, -"and see how it feels to be at your own desk, on your very first job, in one of the most prestigious universities of the world ? Hmmm?"

Kate felt as if the earth were spinning. *How did I ever get myself into this mess? Grammy Lou, where are you now when I need you the most?*

By the time Kate had gotten a grip on herself, Dr. Woodman stood in front of the elevator.

"One last question, Dr. Woodman. Why is it so dirty up here?"

"Well, with the recent budget cuts we've had to get creative here at the library. So we decided to cut our janitorial service by one floor. The fourth floor, darling."

The elevator doors opened and Dr. Woodman stepped in. "The floor where from now on you'll be doing most of your work."

As soon as the elevator doors closed, Kate laid her head down on the desk in front of her and wept.

Chapter Four

The silence on the floor was deafening, save for the intermittent gasps of inhaled breath as Kate sobbed her heart out.

"What did I ever do to deserve all this?" she cried out to no one in particular, except perhaps Grammy Lou, who of course was nowhere even on the planet let alone on the fourth floor of the Charles E. Young Research Library of UCLA.

Well, crap . . .

Like so many times before, Kate soon realized crying wasn't going to change her situation let alone improve it one bit. She wiped her eyes, blew her nose into a table napkin she had lifted from the faculty lounge, and stood to take a more thorough look at her surroundings.

"What a dump!" she said in her most convincing Bette Davis impersonation as she calculated the enormity of the job which lay before her. As far as she could see the first order of business was to get the place cleaned up, if for not the books' and periodicals' sakes, but for her own. Rummaging through her desk, she found paper and pencil and so began a list.

"Cloth rags, buckets, a mop . . ."

Being a product of the foster system Kate learned but a few things yet those she grokked exceptionally well. The most of important was *when everything looks like poop on a stick, get busy and stay busy.* That way one's mind can stay occupied on the activity at hand and not with the direness of the situation.

"window cleaner, furniture polish . . ."

And Kate absolutely refused to see this kink in her career path as anything more than a momentary hiatus before launching forth on what promised to be an exciting and illustrious future as a college librarian. She paused and stared out the window.

Oh my God, who am I kidding? College librarians don't have 'exciting and illustrious careers' unless they end up as serial killers. And little foster girls don't grow up to be useful members of society, no matter how hard they study and work and struggle to get ahead.

"Damn you, Dr. Woodman! And damn you too Randall Carle, you snake! I never should've listened to you in the first place. Whatever made me think I could better myself by getting a PhD and a job position in a college library . . ."

Just then the phone on the desk rang causing Kate to jump nearly out of her skin. The volume had been turned up to the highest setting possible, probably so whoever was working on the floor could hear it should they not be near the desk. Without thinking she grappled for the receiver, anything to stop that obnoxious ringing.

"Hello?"

"*Bon jour*, Kathryn. It is I, Marcel Ricardou."

"Huh? Oh! Hello Professor! Yes, how are you?"

"*Je vais bien, ma chèrie.*" Kate thought she could hear him giggle. "But how are you mademoiselle? Are you enjoying your first day at work?"

"Uh . . . (*ah-choo!*) excuse me . . . um . . . yes, er, oui. It's going . . . well, it's going . . . um . . . well. Yes, it's going well."

"And how do you like your office?"

Kate glanced around as she stood with the receiver against her ear. "Well, it's quite spacious, and I have possibly one of the loveliest views on campus."

Hiccup.

"Ah, *magnifique*! I want to apologize for abandoning you this morning. It's unfortunate, but Roberto and I often squabble over the most inconsequential things. But when we do, we completely forget where we are and who we are with. *Alors,* please forgive me, Kathryn. It won't happen again. I promise.

"But the reason I called is to tell you I've spoken with my wife and we wish to invite you to stay at our home until you can find satisfactory lodging. We've an extra room and would love to have you reside with us as long as you need."

Kate didn't know whether to dance or cry.

Or both.

"Are you sure? I mean, I don't want to impose upon the two of you. And I think I had better confess to you now, I've absolutely no money to my name. That is, until I receive my first pay check. If I survive this job until my first pay check."

"Why, mademoiselle, are you having second thoughts already? It's only the first hour of the first day. Surely things couldn't be as bad as that bad, *n'est pas?*"

"Uh . . ." Kate had to think for a moment. Grammy Lou had always encouraged her no matter how dire the situation to try to look on the bright side—for the silver lining as it were. "Well, I do have a spacious office all to myself, and the view's probably one of the best on campus."

"Ah, *saperlipopette!* Now even I am jealous, dear Kathryn!"

Kate wasn't exactly sure what supper-lee-pop-it meant, but she giggled with the professor as if she went along with his inside joke.

"I will meet you promptly at six. We will then retrieve your car and make our way to my home. Does this sound good to you, *mon amie?*"

"*Absolutement!*" Kate was startled to hear herself speaking French having not had a single lesson in her short life. But sometimes that was how things went. A person picked things up merely by osmosis. Or simply by being in the presence of a strong charismatic personality, and Professor Marcel Ricardou was all that! "I will meet you in front of the library as the chimes toll six."

As soon as Kate hung up the phone she felt noticeably better. Perhaps Grammy Lou was right. Perhaps all she needed was to quit wallowing in this pity-party of hers and start 'blooming where she was planted' and 'keep her sunny side up.' She was tired and worn out from her travels, which was why she was more than likely over-exaggerating the day's difficulties.

Now it was time for her to look at things from a new perspective. She still had her job, two lovely new friends, a place to stay, and a full tummy. And she had a mission—to get this fourth floor monstrosity whipped into shape. Which meant making sure it was spic and span, organized, and with each and every book and periodical repaired and looking their finest. She belonged here, dammit. And she wasn't going to rest until she proved the same to Dr. Woodman as well.

She sat back down at her desk, grasped her pen, and returned to her shopping list.

"a coffee pot, a pound of freshly ground coffee . . ."

She put a line through the last few words.

"make that, two pounds of freshly ground coffee, one hefty mug, and a dust buster . . ."

***

Throughout the entirety of the afternoon all Kate could think about was Professor Roberto Cassinelli and his beautiful face. And of course his tight pants, especially as they pulled across his upper thighs. *Lordy! This floor is certainly beginning to warm up!*

Not having her cleaning supplies as of yet, Kate decided at the very least to get the books, journals and periodicals organized into neat stacks, placing those which needed the most attention closest to her working desk and those needing the least further back. She was no dummy. But Kate had long been aware her skills as a librarian weren't necessarily about her intelligence and scholarly aptitude, but more about her predilection toward detail and organization.

She also liked to have things very clean and germ free. Actually, if the truth were known, more than one OCD feature showed up in Kate's mental health makeup. And she clearly understood it was because of these features that becoming a librarian seemed like the best career choice at the time. Yet, something about the profession also struck as something untrue to her adventurous soul.

"I mean, let's face it. This job's boring!" She said out loud to no one except herself. So to make the work less tedious, Kate continued to fantasize over her new Italian dreamboat. As she toddled over to her first stack of damaged periodicals, she imagined floating in a gondola along a quiet Venetian canal snuggled in the arms of this long eye-lashed hunk.

'La mia bella, Katerina! How delicious you look tonight!'
'Oh, thank you, Roberto. You don't look so bad yourself!'

She picked up the stack and struggled to carry it close to her desk.

'Your lips are like soft rose petals from which I wish to suck their heavenly sweetness.'

'How nice of you to notice.'

'May I, darling?'

'Uh...'

Kate dropped the dated journals with a thud.

Ah-choo!

Kate wiped her dusty hands on her skirt and continued her process, only this time with a stack of oversized reference books, far too heavy to carry in one trip, but which she attempted all the same. As she stumbled across the expanse of the library floor, her thoughts took her back to Professor Cassinelli. Kate now imagined the two of them sitting at dusk in a diminutive outdoor trattoria in the heart of the Uffizi Piazza in Florence, Italy.

'Come, la mia patatina, my little potato, open your mouth and let me feed you a taste of this delicious gelato al limon.'

'But I have my own gelato, Roberto, and can feed myself.'

'But, no, Katerina. I want to be the one to feed you—to place the delicate flavors of my country into your mouth to savor.'

'Uh . . .'

'That's it! Open wide . . .'

'Oh, dear, I think some of your gelato al limon is running

down my chin!'

'Ah! You are right, my little mouse, la mia topolina! Here, let me lick it off!'

Instantly the books plummeted and scattered everywhere.

Hiccup!

"Damn! Damn! Damn!" Kate said out loud as on her hands and knees she searched feverishly for the texts one by one. "Just when things were getting good!"

'Don't run away from me, la mia farfallina, my little butterfly. Playing hard to get only makes me want you that much more.'

'I'm not trying to get away from you. I merely wanted to pick up these books and—

'Forget the books, bambolina. Come, let me hold you in my arms. Let me kiss your adorable mouth. Let me touch your breasts and run my fingers across your . . .'

Kate face planted onto the cold cement floor.

Ah-choo! Hiccup! Ah-choo!

Perhaps it was best not to preoccupy her mind quite so energetically with imaginings of her and Roberto. Although Kate enjoyed thinking about him no end, she had to admit her thoughts of him were slowing her down and causing her to make her already filthy clothes even dirtier. Plus, being so physically attracted to the man so early in their acquaintanceship was wrecking havoc on her hormones and leaving her more anxious than could be considered normally healthy.

It had been Kate's habit in the past, whenever she found herself getting too carried away by her fantasy life, the mere act of counting seemed to pull her back into reality—mundane though it be. Not knowing what else to do, she opted to do just that for the remainder of the day—to count books and periodicals as she moved them from one spot to another, organizing them according to her own criteria and future plans.

In fact, by the time six o'clock came around, Kate figured she had placed more than seven thousand books and forty-five hundred journals and periodicals into neat logical piles. Tomorrow morning she planned to devote to cleaning so that by noon she could begin to repair the first of her many damaged texts—one scraped, scratched and shredded victim at a time.

***

Marcel had stared at his watch for the last few hours, waiting for time to pass quickly so he could finally meet up with Kate and apologize once again for his earlier rudeness. He felt so bitterly ashamed of himself he had called his wife to tell her what he had done and to ask for her wisdom and professional advice.

After all, she had once been a successful psychiatrist

of considerable note when they lived in London, the city of her birth. Cecily Higgenbottom Ricardou was as thoroughly English as her dear Marcel was French! In fact, she drank her cuppa Yorkshire Tea with the same ardor and zeal as her husband smoked his precious Galois cigarettes.

Yet Marcel was always hesitant to call home from work. He never liked to interrupt his wife's daily activities, but especially with a phone call which could easily frighten her into thinking he may be in danger or going through some kind of medical emergency. Today however he had no choice. Roberto had once again gotten under his skin, and as a result Marcel had totally lost his cool. So much so, that he had momentarily forgotten about Doctor Kathryn Richards, his new friend and colleague. *Mon Dieu!*

The phone rang once, twice, three times. Marcel was tempted to hang up with each second that passed. Finally, his wife picked up.

"Hello? Marcel, is that you? Is anything the matter?"

The terror in Cecily's voice confirmed Marcel's earlier reservations. "*No, mon amour.* I'm fine. Don't worry so. I'm calling merely to ask a special favor."

Marcel hoped the added warmth in his voice would allay his wife's initial fears. They had always looked out for one another. But now that they were getting older, it seemed to Marcel that Cecily was even more anxious about their combined health and safety. Marcel was all Cecily had and so she doted on him. And he on her as well.

"Please don't tell me you wish to work late again tonight. I've a lovely roast in the oven and . . ."

"No, no, no, *ma chérie*. I will be home at the usual time. *Mais,* if it's all right with you, I would like to invite a new colleague for dinner. She's so young and so very frightened. And as far as I can tell, all alone in this world . . ."

Cecily sighed and then giggled into the receiver. "Again

you've found a little lost sparrow, haven't you Marcel?"

It was true. Over the years Marcel had made it his mission to help new staff and faculty become situated in the university community until they felt comfortable and somewhat established. "Oui, I suppose I have. And from what I can already surmise, this one is the most sparrow-like of all the baby birds that have graced our lives thus far, Cecily."

"Then we must do what we've agreed upon. Invite the little lost one for dinner, and I will ready the spare bedroom. And what's our new boarder's name?"

"Kate. Actually, Dr. Kathryn Richards. Unfortunately she's working for that ogre Marian Woodman in the research library. I doubt she'll last any longer than the others who've recently passed under that vulture's eye, but while she does, I want Kate to know she's well liked and appreciated for who she is."

"Oh, Marcel. It has been so long since we've had a little girl in our home." Try as they may, Marcel and Cecily had remained childless throughout their forty years of marriage. "Yes, yes, yes. Thank you, darling. Already I forgive you for calling and scaring me half out of my skin. Now, hang up so I can get things ready for our new guest!"

And so the conversation had gone—which was absolutely the right amount of encouragement for Marcel to get in touch with Kate and invite her to his home.

Chapter Five

Marcel packed his brief case, crawled into his trench coat, and positioned his beret jauntily over his balding head in anticipation for the campus chimes tolling six. He glanced for the thousandth time at the clock on his office wall. He still had fifteen minutes before he needed to leave in order to meet Kate at their appointed hour.

So he paced.

And he paced some more.

And he continued pacing for what seemed like an eternity before looking back up at the clock for the one thousand and oneth time. He rolled his eyes and sighed.

"*C'est tout!*" he blurted out as he hammered his fist into his forehead. "That's it! I can wait no longer."

He flew out his second floor office, slamming the door behind him. Taking two stairs at a time, Marcel then sped out of the building toward the library. He loved this time of the evening when on campus most of the student population had thinned out and the earlier sequestered faculty took to the sidewalks either to catch a city bus or find their cars in one of the campus parking garages.

Only a hand full of staff and faculty walked home, as so few affordable homes bordered the campus. Not that those who worked at the college were underpaid, but the houses in the surrounding neighborhoods of Westwood, Brentwood and Bel Air were exorbitantly expensive. Luckily, Marcel and Cecily had purchased their house several years before prices skyrocketed. Granted their home was on the small side, what with two bedrooms and one bath.

Yet, above the single car garage the couple had built a one-room apartment so as to lodge their visiting families from Paris or London. Now, however, with both sets of parents gone, Marcel and Cecily kept the apartment empty for prospective tenants like Kate—lost, lonely, and broke—who needed a hand up in getting back up on their feet.

The sky had nearly turned dark when Marcel saw what he thought might be Kate standing in front of the library's outdoor cement stairs. The woman's silhouette indeed seemed to be like Kate, but the creature's clothing was so soiled and her face besmudged, that Marcel couldn't help but wonder if this was the same woman he had breakfasted with.

He stopped for a second and squinted at the solitary figure before him.

"Kathryn," he shouted, "is that you?"

"Yoo-hoo, Marcel." Kate shouted back as she waved a free arm. "It's me all right. Kate."

Marcel felt a tinge of worry yet smiled all the same.

"So it is you after all," he exclaimed as he neared her. "You look as if you've put in a day at the gravel pit rather than a college research library. *Mon Dieu!* What in the world have you been doing?"

"Well . . ." Kate hesitated at first, but then as she linked her arm into his, she did her best to give her newfound friend an update. While the two of them strolled to where she had parked her car, Kate rattled on as Marcel listened. He was immediately floored by what he heard.

"I can't believe Dr. Woodman would be so cruel as to exile you to the top floor and force you to do a job which you're obviously overqualified to do. The woman has overstepped her authority and must be reprimanded."

Marcel gently patted Kate's hand as he spoke.

Kate's face turned ashen. "Please don't say anything, Marcel. I don't want to start any trouble. Besides, I'm actually eager to learn something new and to prove I can do it as well as anyone else. I truly want to get back into Dr. Woodman's good graces, but I think this is the best way to do just that."

"If you're sure then . . ."

"I am, Marcel. Thank you anyway for your concern."

Marcel wasn't as yet convinced being quiet was the correct answer to Dr Woodman's behavior, but he wasn't going to share his trepidation with Kate, for at that particular moment the two of them arrived where they had left Kate's parked VW Bug earlier that morning.

Unbelievably, the parking slot was empty.

For several seconds the two of them stared into the vacant lot, trying with some difficulty to compute the information being given. Or not given, as the case of the missing car may be.

Kate was the first to speak. "Marcel, do you not see what I don't see?"

Marcel blinked purposely twice before looking around the lot with the hope of seeing the car miraculously appear before his eyes.

"*Oui mademoiselle*, I do not see what you don't see as well."

"Are you sure we're in the correct place? I mean maybe the Volkswagen is in some other lot and we've simply forgotten which one." Kate was fishing like mad.

Breaking apart, they each circled the empty parking slot looking for any scrap of evidence confirming that Kate's car had indeed been sitting in the very spot it now clearly wasn't.

"I'm sorry, Kathryn. But I'm sure this is where we

last saw your car." Marcel scoured the ground while Kate's eyes searched from one end of the lot to the other.

"I am, too, but I had to ask the most obvious question nonetheless."

Marcel bent over and picked up what appeared to be one of his campus business cards. Turning it over he saw it was the note he had placed on the car's windshield should the campus parking police be tempted to ticket or tow away Kate's car.

"*Je suis désolé, mademoiselle.* I'm now positive this is where we left your car this morning."

As Kate neared her friend, she felt hot tears forming in her eyes. *Don't you dare start crying! Don't do it! STOP!*

Kate stared at the card she now held in her hand and wept like a banshee.

"Oh, Kathryn, I'm so sorry! Yet, I'm sure your car is perfectly safe. The parking police more than likely didn't see my note and towed your car to the impound yard not far from here."

By now Kate was crying so loudly Marcel was unsure as to what to do next. Put his arms around her? Pat her on the head? Offer her his last handkerchief? Without warning Kate leaned her forehead onto his chest and let out all the frustrations of the day in one fell swoop.

Soaking his trench coat with her tears, Kate didn't stop until she had transferred all her makeup and runny nose droppings onto Marcel's front. Carefully he placed his chubby arms around Kate's fragile body and waited for her to finish.

Which after some time she finally did.

"Oh, Professor. I'm afraid I've ruined your coat," Kate said looking into his comforting face. "I'll pay to have it cleaned. I promise. Just as soon as I get my pay-hay-hay che-heh-heh-heck!"

Kate burst out crying one last time before accepting Marcel's last handkerchief to wipe her eyes.

"Now you listen to me, Kathryn. We can easily walk to my house and call the campus police from there. Then we'll make arrangements to pick up your Volkswagen and bring it back to your new home. *N'est pas?*"

"My new home?" Kate wasn't sure she heard him right.

"Yes, *oui*. Your new home. Madame Ricardou and I want you to come live with us. You'll have your own space above our garage for as long as you like."

"But I can't afford . . ."

"Now, now, don't you worry about all that. After a few paychecks, then we can talk about rent. But for now please accept our heartfelt invitation."

Kate didn't know whether to hug the little round man for joy or cry like a baby again on his already dampened shoulder. So instead she blew her nose into the clean white handkerchief she held in her hand and thought how lucky she was to have such good friends as Marcel and his wife. Without the two of them, she knew she would be lost.

***

Kate was silent as the two of them strolled the few remaining blocks to the Ricardou home. To get her mind off her problems of the day Kate once again fantasized what an evening out would be like with the handsome Roberto Cassinelli as her date. That is, if she ever got the chance to do more than merely attend an evening's film club presentation. *Last Year at Marienbad*. The title alone sounded rather grim. But Kate was up for whatever excuse she needed to get better acquainted with the handsome Italian professor. *Ah-choo!*

"*Alors, mademoiselle*, we're at last here."

"Huh?"

"Welcome to my home, Kathryn. It isn't much by

California standards, but it's filled with love and a most comfortable extra bed." The little professor smiled warmly as he patted Kate's hand. "Come. Let's go in. I want to do meet my dear wife."

From the outside the Ricardou house seemed no bigger than a thimble. But once the door opened, Kate felt the cozy warmth and calm of a home filled with art, books, music and an overweight cat ooze out from its wallpapered *trompe l'oeil* walls.

The very air itself was heavy with the aroma of whatever it was Mrs. Ricardou was cooking for dinner.

"Is that you Marcel?" came a voice from where the odor emanated.

"*Oui, ma chérie.* Sorry we're late, but we had a bit of a mishap with Mademoiselle Kathryn's automobile."

Immediately a little round woman in a flowered apron came bustling around the corner, feverishly wiping her hands on a dish towel as she traveled.

"Bloody Hell! You weren't in an accident, were you? Please tell me you're not hurt!"

Marcel barely managed to help Kate remove her jacket before greeting his wife with outstretched arms. "Now Cecily, there's no need for you to worry. Professor Kathryn and I are safe and sound. But unfortunately the same can't be said for her Volkswagen Bug, which appears to have vanished from the face of the earth." He then winked at Kate as he hugged his wife to his chest.

"A Bug?" Cecily sniffled, her eyes wet with tears.

"Yes," Kate barged in. "The Volkswagen Convertible's my car. Or was my car, until it most inconveniently disappeared."

"*Ma chérie*, may I introduce Doctor Kathryn Richards, our new campus research librarian."

"Enchantez, Doctor Richards!" exclaimed Cecily as

she quickly blew her nose into the already well-used kitchen towel.

"Please call me Kate, Madame Ricardou," she said as she extended her hand.

"How lovely to meet you too, Kate. And please, call me Cecily." The woman immediately took Kate's hand into her own warm moist hands. "Forgive me for my outburst, but I can't help but worry about Marcel. He is and has always been my rock. My anchor."

Kate smiled at the gentle and honest hospitality of the woman who held her hand as if clamped in a vice.

"And I'm so sorry for your loss," added Cecily.

"My loss?" Kate questioned as she peeked over at Marcel.

"Ah, Cecily's referring to your missing car," the professor quickly added while hanging up his overcoat. "So, please, have a seat while I call the campus police. They should be able to tell me where they've had it towed."

"Can I get you something to drink, Kate?" Cecily asked as she moved toward the kitchen.

A whiskey would be nice!

"Uh . . . I'd love a cup of tea."

"Ah!" Cecily smiled at Kate. "Brilliant!"

As Cecily scooted into the kitchen, Kate glanced over at Marcel and saw he was already on the phone. And if her ears served her right, he was speaking in what she would call harsh tones. Since his back was to her, Kate cautiously moved closer to get within hearing range.

"That's correct. Dr. Kathryn Richards parked her VW Bug in the visitor's lot early this morning, and when we returned to pick it up, the car was gone. Now, did you tow it to the impound lot or did you not? We need to know so we can retrieve it as soon as possible!"

Marcel must've sensed Kate's presence, because he

then turned to face her, his hand over the phone receiver.

"Campus Security is checking. Imbeciles!"

Kate watched the little professor wipe his brow with yet another clean handkerchief, this one appearing from his pants' pocket. A part of her was obviously upset over the disappearance of her car. Yet, at the same time she couldn't help but find the entire string of events as somewhat comical. In other words, she didn't know whether to laugh or cry—which, as she thought about it, was on more than one occasion her normal state of behavior.

"Thank you, Marcel," she said and smiled sweetly.

Marcel returned her smile. And was about to say something when his attention was taken back to the phone. "Yes?"

Kate noted the pause as he listened.

"What? That cannot be!" Marcel blanched. "How could that have happened?"

Another pause.

"Yes . . . yes . . . I'll tell her. Thank you for your help."

Silently Marcel hung up the phone. Anxious for the professor to speak, Kate pulled on his suit jacket.

"So, what did they say? Do they have my car?"

"Mademoiselle Kathryn, I regret to tell you your Volkswagen Bug has unfortunately been stolen."

Kate merely stared at him unable at first to take in his words.

She then released her longest sigh of the day.

Well, shit! Welcome to L.A. Dr. Richards!

Chapter Six

Despite the immediacy of her current devastation, Kate enjoyed the lovely meal Cecily had prepared. Roast chicken, baby peas, and a creamy potato and onion casserole completed the menu, fully satisfying Kate's overly-stretched appetite. It had been a long time if ever since Kate had been fussed over with the same exuberance for life which both Marcel and Cecily exhibited.

But, even though she listened and conversed with the two of them throughout dinner, somewhere in the back of her mind she couldn't help but think about the handsome Roberto Cassinelli. And the absolute impossibility of such a jewel of a man ever becoming a more prominent fixture in her life.

She was about to be served a dessert of fruit and assorted cheeses, when there was a knock at the door.

"Who in the world could that be?" asked Cecily as Marcel stood and made his way toward the door.

"Perhaps it's the police?" Tossed back Marcel as he reached for the doorknob.

Kate was grateful Marcel had called the police to report her stolen car. The patrolman in charge had warned Marcel and Kate the chances of finding her car were probably zero to none. However, it didn't hurt to keep a positive attitude and to still hope beyond hope thought Kate.

"Buona sera, Katerina!" A voice bellowed from outside the front door.

Kate's heart leapt into her throat.

Did that policeman just call me what I think he called me?

Ah-choo!

Standing in the threshold of the door stood not a policeman but Roberto, the man of her dreams, and not only that—he was calling her the very name from her fantasy.

Ah-choo!

"Bless you!"

"A tes souhaits!"

"Salute!"

... retorted Cecily, Marcel and Roberto respectively.

Kate blew her nose into her napkin. "Thank you, merci, and grazie!" she answered as she placed the soiled serviette next to her plate.

"Who's at the door, Marcel?' asked Cecily eagerly. It wasn't every day she and Marcel had company, let alone two unplanned guests in a row.

Playfully Marcel shrugged his shoulders. "No one

special. Merely Roberto and that alien dog of his!"

Before he could shut the door on Roberto, the handsome Italian stuck his foot in the door.

"Now, Marcel," he chuckled. "You know very well Mr. Steed's a pug, not an extraterrestrial. And I haven't come to have you insult my dog, Professor Grumpy Pants, but rather to see if Katerina would like an escort to our French Film Club meeting."

Once again Kate's heart fluttered. She closed her eyes and in her mind she saw herself accepting Roberto's barrage of amorous licks, nips and kisses.

> *'Oh, my darling Katerina. You are so beautiful! Your hair, your eyes, your lips.'*
> *'Thank you, Roberto.'*
> *'You're welcome, my little kitten. (kiss, kiss, kiss) I want nothing more than to ravish your body, il mia piccola gattina, starting with that lovely neck of yours!'*

Hiccup!

"Kathryn?" *Cecily? What's she doing here in my fantasy? Go away!*

"Kathryn, are you all right?" asked Cecily

"Huh?" Kate grunted, the heat of embarrassment rising in her cheeks. "Oh, yes. Sorry. It's been a long day." Kate worked without success at slowing down her racing heart. "I'm fine. Honest!"

Marcel turned back to face his friend. "I'm sorry, but Kathryn has had a time of it today and perhaps would feel better to stay in for the evening. Perhaps next week she will want to attend."

"Actually, Marcel, I feel perfectly fine!" she said as she stood. Kate was grateful now that earlier Cecily had offered a dress and sweater to change into after her quick shower. Although the length of the hem was shorter than she normally liked to wear, the dress did show off her curvaceous figure and shapely legs.

"Are you sure, Kathryn? I believe Roberto would

understand if you didn't want to go out tonight."

Kate swallowed hard. What she wanted to do was run out the door, grab Roberto, throw him to the ground and sit on his face. On the other hand, the Ricardous had been more than gracious, and she didn't want to do anything to insult their generosity or hurt their feelings.

"Uhm . . ."

"Yes?"

"Oui?"

"Si?"

—the three asked as they turned their heads to stare.

Hiccup!

"I think I'll be all right. As long as I'm with Roberto, that is."

"Hrrrmph!" exclaimed Marcel. "That's all I needed to hear!"

Kate sighed with relief.

"Let me get my coat and we'll all walk there together!" Marcel said as he turned to retrieve his signature trench coat from the hall closet.

Kate's breath hitched in her throat.

"That is not necessary, Marcel." Roberto cut in. "Signorina Katerina is more than safe with me."

Kate wasn't sure but she thought Roberto wiggled his eyebrows.

"Oh!" Cecily chirped. Like Kate she too had seen Roberto's attempt at flirting.

"Everything's fine, ma chérie." Marcel said, calming Cecily's nerves. "No need to worry yourself. Kate and I won't be out late. Gratefully *Last Year at Marienbad* runs but ninety minutes, which is about all a person can take of that miserable excuse of an actor, Albertazzi!"

"Watch it, Marcel!" warned Roberto. "Or you will be making a necessary stop at the ER sooner than think!"

Roberto chuckled at his witticism, but Kate clearly saw that underneath his polite veneer the Italian stud-muffin meant business.

Marcel was about to retaliate when Kate stepped over to her chubby French friend and linked her arm through his. "*Allons-y,* Marcel. Let's go!"

"I won't be late, darling," Marcel blurted as Kate rushed him out the door.

"And I'll make sure of that!" added Kate as the odd couple spilled out into the front yard. Roberto with Mr. Steed followed close behind, making room for Cecily who now stood at the door waving goodbye.

"I'll wait up, Marcel. And make sure he has fun, Kathryn. Marcel can be a complete moron, un *complètement débile,* when he's bored."

Kate was about to put Cecily's mind at ease when she suddenly became aware of a rather peculiar looking man standing in the front yard, smiling at her and holding a leash connected to an equally strange looking black pug.

"Good evening, Marcel. Katerina, Roberto told me we were making a new friend this evening, but I never imagined she would be as lovely as your escort!"

"Gah!" Kate was at a loss for words.

Who the hell is this? And what's he doing here?

"Ah, Katerina. I see you have met my partner, Chuck." Roberto said cheerfully.

"Err . . ."

The husky Wally-Shawn-look-alike stepped forward and offered his hand. "Enchantez, Katerina."

Clearly flummoxed, Kate stood motionless.

"Partner?' she asked.

"Husband, actually," answered the gnome.

Roberto put his arm around Chuck and kissed him on the top of his balding head. "*Sí, mio marito!*" Robert added lovingly. "And at his feet is the lovely sister to Mr. Steed, our Emma Peel."

"Say 'hi' to Katerina, Emma," commanded Chuck.

"Woof!" barked Emma.

"Woof! Woof!" added Mr. Steed.

Kate at last found her voice. "So, you're . . . uh . . . you're . . . errrr . . ."

"Gay!" Chuck and Roberto shouted simultaneously.

Ah, ssshhhhiiiiittttt!

Ah-choo!

Hiccup!

Ah-choo! Hiccup!! Aaaahhhh-chooooooo!

"Are you all right, Kathryn? Do you need another handkerchief or an antacid tablet perhaps?" Marcel quietly asked.

"Yes. I mean, no. I mean . . . oh, I don't know what I mean! What I mean to say is . . . ah, congratulations. Yes, congratulations, and not necessarily because you're gay, although that's nice too, but that you've found each other. That Mr. Steed and Emma have such a loving home. And uh . . . that uh . . . er . . ."

"It is a shock, Katerina, I know," said Roberto. "But the time, she is flying by. And if we do not get moving, we will be late for the film. So, shall we go, yes?"

"Lead the way, Roberto!" answered Chuck enthusiastically.

The two forged ahead with Mr. Steed and Emma Peel in tow.

"You look noticeably disappointed, Mademoiselle Kathryn," whispered Marcel in her ear. "Would you feel better if we stayed at home instead? I know I would."

"No, no Marcel. I'm okay. Just a little discombobulated is all," said Kate. "I think once the movie starts I will feel better. Back to my old self!"

Whoever the hell that is!

"Are you sure?" pressed Marcel.

"Yes, of course. *Allons-y!*"

"*Absolutement! Allons-y!* Let's go!" Marcel placed his hand on Kate's, her arm still linked through his. It took nearly everything she had within her not to tear up and cry. But Kate quickly reminded herself this was but a mere disappointment and not the end of the world. Besides, she was in the company of new friends and good people. So why be sad?

HWAAAAH!

***

Marcel had been right. *Last Year at Marienbad* was as miserable as Kate felt, although she did find Giorgio Albertazzi rather sexy in a geeky, too-smart-for-his-own-face kind of way. Yet, all through the movie Kate's mind wandered.

Why in the world would Roberto want to be married to Chuck when he could have me?

She really should hate Chuck.

I mean, how dare he encroach upon my fantasy?!

Yet, as the evening progressed, Kate found the man absolutely endearing. Chuck was attentive to Steed and Mrs. Peel, far more so than Roberto, and at the same time charming and polite to both her and Marcel. In fact, by the time the film ended, Kate was hanging on Chuck's every word, completely ignoring Roberto's antics.

The moment the film ended Roberto flew out of his seat and flipped on the way-too-bright florescent lights of the room. "So, *Mesdames et Messieurs*, was that not the best of our film series yet this term?"

"Not!" Chuck whispered to Kate. "I think if I have to see that dreadful movie one more time, I'll commit myself."

Kate snickered.

"Did I hear someone disapprove?" Roberto asked the club's membership.

"Here we go!" said Marcel to no one in particular.

Kate couldn't help but notice Roberto's face turning a rather dark shade of scarlet.

"Marcel! If you have something to say, then say it here and now in front of us all!"

Luckily Marcel didn't take Roberto's bait. Instead he merely smiled and took a moment before replying.

"Roberto, this isn't the time nor the place to fight over such a silly thing as a film," Marcel said gently.

"Did I hear you call my favorite movie of all time 'silly'? Roberto said as he clenched his fists at his sides. Everyone immediately grew quiet as the tension in the room escalated.

"Come up here Marcel, now! And let's have this out once and for all!"

Kate watched as Marcel did his best to remain calm, but even she wasn't sure what he would do if Roberto continued to badger him. After a few calculated seconds, Marcel finally spoke.

"Please, Roberto. I don't want to fight you. So stop acting the buffoon!"

A collective gasp went up as everyone in the room held their breath.

"'Buffoon'? *You* of all people dare call *me* a 'buffoon'? I'll show you who's a *buffoon*!" Instantly Roberto rushed toward where Marcel and Kate were sitting.

"Eke!" Kate screamed as Marcel flew out of this chair.

"THAT'S ENOUGH, ROBERTO! STOP WHERE YOU ARE AND DON'T YOU DARE MOVE AN INCH!" a voice bellowed above the noise in the room.

Roberto stopped abruptly as if he had run into a brick wall.

Kate didn't remember exactly how she had gotten out of her chair and over to where Marcel was standing, but there she stood in front of the little Frenchman as if to protect him from Roberto's assault.

"Stay out of this, Chuck. This is between me and Marcel and has nothing to do with you!"

With his eyes staring intensely into Roberto's, Chuck carefully ambled toward him as he spoke.

"No, Roberto. You're wrong. This has everything to do with me. *You* and me both—together."

"What are you saying?"

Kate was sure she saw Roberto flinch.

"I am as tired of your bullying as I am of seeing this film! It's obvious to me not everyone enjoys it as much as you do, Roberto. Actually, very few of us here in the club do. But never for a second should we be afraid of speaking our opinions, even if they're contrary to your own."

Roberto stiffened. "Perhaps it is time for you to leave."

Marcel leaned forward and whispered in Kate's ear. "I think it's time for *us* to make our exit as well, *n'est pas?*"

Chuck took a step forward, causing Steed and Mrs. Peel to cower even further under Chuck's chair.

"No, Roberto, I think it's you who must go before you make even bigger ass of yourself than you already have."

Kate inhaled sharply as Roberto stepped into Chuck's space, the two men now chest to chest.

"*Esci* Get out!!" Roberto seethed as he pushed Chuck, nearly causing the man to fall on his butt. Like lightning, however, Chuck regained his footing and charged toward Roberto full force.

As soon as the top of Chuck's head met Roberto's stomach, the room cleared, leaving only Marcel and Kate along with Steed and Mrs. Peel to witness. Soon both men were wrestling on the floor, screaming obscenities in both perfect English and exquisite Italian.

"I suspect you're right, Marcel. Now would be a very good time for us to leave!"

Not wanting to leave the pugs behind, Kate motioned for Marcel to grab Mrs. Peel's lead as she did the same for Steed. The four of them then tiptoed quietly out the door as folding chairs flew above their heads and crashed around them.

"Is it always like this between those two?" asked Kate.

"No, not always. But unfortunately often enough for us at the film club to know when to make our escape."

For a brief second Kate entertained the thought that if perhaps Roberto and Chuck broke up, the Italian would be free to date her instead. But as soon as that thought entered her mind, it disappeared into the night air. And what a lovely night it was, thought Kate. Not too cold or too warm—a sweater-wearing night, complete with a clear sky and thousands of sparkling stars.

"You've had quite the day for yourself, *oui* Mademoiselle Kathryn?"

"*Oui*, Marcel, quite a day indeed!"

Chapter Seven

Not a word was spoken between the two of them as they strolled their way back home. Marcel scratched his brain for what to say to cheer Kathryn up, to give her some kind of comfort, but in the end he was at a loss. At least the walk was a short one.

No sooner had Marcel unlocked the front door, but Cecily dressed in her robe and slippers was there to meet him. "My, but you two are back early? I didn't expect you for at least another hour." She said as she helped Marcel with his coat.

Marcel smiled. Not only did his dear Cecily worry whenever he was five minutes late, but also when he was an hour early.

"The meeting ended rather abruptly so we took our leave," he said.

Kate wandered over to the nearby baseboard heater to warm her slightly chilled behind and legs. "Actually, Roberto and Chuck fell into a disagreement—a fist fight, to be exact," she blurted.

"Bloody hell!" screeched Cecily. "Are you all right, Marcel? Roberto didn't strike you, did he?"

Marcel pulled Cecily into his arms. "No, no, *ma chérie*. He wouldn't dare!" And he kissed the top of her head.

At first Kate giggled quietly but then broke out into a full belly laugh. "Funny, all through that boring movie I was wondering how we could possibly escape. Then as soon as the fight started, I found myself wanting to stay. Lordy, that's the most excitement I've had in some time!"

Marcel smiled in agreement. "*D'accord!* Roberto isn't a

violent man, except when it comes to his obsession with that ridiculous film. Then he becomes *un fou, un lunatic!*"

"Agreed. I don't think he's dangerous either," Kate added. "Merely passionate. You know how Italians can be. I think that's what makes them so attractive. More often than not they move and speak from their hearts, and not necessarily from their heads."

Marcel nodded and sighed. "Ah, perhaps that's why I'm so fond of him. Roberto's a man of deep feeling."

"And excessive charm!" piped in Cecily. "Now, why don't I make us all a cup of hot chocolate before bed? To calm us down and warm us up."

"Ah, *merveilleux!*" exclaimed Marcel as he kissed his wife once again, this time on her cheek. His eyes followed her lovingly as she slipped into the kitchen.

"You know, Marcel, your wife's absolutely lovely! And so very kind, too. Like you!"

Marcel turned his attention back to his new boarder. "I think instead it's a case of beauty and the beast!" he snickered. "But you're correct. Cecily's my everything. Why she has put up with me all these years is a true mystery."

"Yes, but who doesn't love a good mystery now and then! Besides, I think you're nothing less than a romantic as well!" Kate added as she spied the numerous books standing at attention on the built-in bookshelves encircling the teeny living room. "You certainly seem to own quite a few British mysteries—Arthur Conan Doyle, Raymond Chandler, G. K. Chesterton, A. E. Mason, and, oh, my favorite, Agatha Christie."

"Yes, most of them belong to Cecily. As a psychiatrist she has found them to be a great resource, especially in understanding the inner workings of the criminal mind," Marcel explained. "She has actually written several articles on the correlation between villains portrayed in fiction and those in real life."

Marcel was obviously proud of his wife, not only for her professional expertise and accomplishments, but for her sweet concern for him. Not to mention her cooking.

"Here we are!" announced Cecily as if on cue, carrying a tray with three steaming mugs of cocoa topped with oodles of whipping cream. "Let's sit in the living room, shall we?"

Kate helped herself to one of the fragrant brews and made her way toward the cozy looking sofa. Marcel did the same before plopping into his favorite overstuffed leather chair. Finally, Cecily joined Kate on the other end of the family's leather Chesterfield. As if in perfect tempo, the three slurped their hot chocolates in unison.

"Mmmmm!" moaned Kate. "This is divine!"

"Oh, thank you," said Cecily. "Family recipe, you know."

"You've outdone yourself once again, *ma chérie*." Marcel said licking the whip from off the top of his moustache. "Just the way I like it!"

The three took a second long slurp again in unison.

"So," said Kate to Cecily, "Marcel tells me you're a reader. I'm a librarian, so I'm always curious as to what people read and why."

Cecily's entire face brightened, her eyes sparkling with curiosity. "Why, so am I my dear! Ever since I was a young child I've been attracted to the mysteries of the human mind. I suppose that's what has attracted me to detective fiction, particularly of the British kind. And yourself?"

Marcel watched as Kate searched her memory. "Well, I'm really quite fond of the Agatha Christie's novels. Hercule Poirot's one of my heroes."

"Ah, mine too!" chimed in Marcel. "In fact, it isn't a stretch of the imagination to see should I had not become a university professor, I most certainly would've been a detective with the Paris Sûreté!"

Cecily coughed, nearly choking on her cocoa. "Thanks be to God you did not, Marcel. For if you had, I surely wouldn't have survived beyond the first day of our courtship!"

"*Alors,* there you have it!" Marcel said with a wink. "A choice well made on my part!"

Kate licked the last of the whipping cream from her now empty mug. "It's been quite a day for me to say the least. So if you don't mind, I think I had better go to bed. But first, if you could recommend one of your novels for me to read, Cecily, I would deeply appreciative it."

"Oh! Well, have you ever read one of Ms. Christie's Jane Marple stories?" Cecily asked as she stood. "I find them particularly insightful."

"Gosh, I guess I haven't. At least I don't remember…"

Cecily reached up and pulled a thin leather-bound novel from her shelf. "Try this one my dear. It's one of my favorites, and a good choice for a novice's first Miss Marple adventure."

Kate perused the cover. "*Sleeping Murder*—well, that's quite a title. You promise this book won't keep me awake?"

"Just remember to focus on the 'sleeping' part of the title," jested Marcel, "and less on the word 'murder'."

Kate hugged Cecily and then went to Marcel's chair and kissed him on the top of his warm head. She then took the apartment key from out of her purse and headed for the front door.

"Good night, you two," she said turning. "I can't thank you enough for making me feel so welcomed into your home. I promise you, as soon as I can, I will pay every cent of the rent I owe."

"Don't worry about all that now, Kathryn. Sleep well,

and we will see you in the morning for *un petit dejeuner.*" Marcel stood and took his wife's hand.

"Yes, a full English breakfast." Cecily added excitedly, "complete with coddled eggs, fried kidneys, black pudding and kippered salmon!" Cecily added with excitement.

Marcel couldn't help but notice Kate's face turning gray.

"Well, er, that sounds, uh, lovely!" Kate said as she hurried out the door.

As soon as the door clicked shut, Cecily gazed up into her husband's eyes. "Thank you for bringing Kathryn home to us, Marcel. I do believe a part of me has fallen in love with her already."

Marcel gently guided Cecily toward their bedroom. "I feel the same way, ma chérie. How lucky we are, n'est pas?"

"Mais oui!"

***

Kate had no sooner shut the door than she began to sneeze.

Ah-choo!

And hiccup.

Hiccup!

Normally she had nothing more than a cup of coffee in the morning, but tomorrow was the beginning of a new chapter in her life. So no matter how sick to her stomach she felt now, somehow she would find a way to not only share breakfast with these two very sweet people, but enjoy it as well!

Kate washed and scrubbed her face with a lovely Crabtree & Evelyn Rose soap. She then slipped into the pair of borrowed pajamas Cecily had found for her from Marcel's dresser drawer—complete with a over-sized *M* monogrammed on the front pocket—and poured herself into her new bed.

"Ahhh! This is heaven!" she sighed as she slid between the pink satin sheets. A nearly full harvest moon shone in through a tiny nearby octagonal window, lighting the room only enough to see in spite of the dark.

Not even twenty-four hours had passed since her arrival in Los Angles, and yet more had happened to her that single half day than all the other accumulated days of her life. She had met the man of her dreams. Granted he was unavailable in more ways than one, but still . . .

She had also begun the job of her dreams, except her boss turned out to be nothing less than a complete nightmare. And to be honest, even the job itself sucked. She had her car stolen along with her belongings (such as they were), and the chance to join a campus club and meet new friends ended in much the same way—a disaster!

No, Kate thought to herself, this was not the club, nor

the job, nor the stolen car, nor the man of her dreams kind of day! But as she lay in bed staring at the moonlit sky she was grateful beyond measure for having met both Cecily and Marcel—the parents she had wished for as a child but never had. They were warm and sweet, smart and wise—everything she could've ever wanted in a mother and father.

A warm tear rolled down her cheek as she thought of Grammy Lou and how proud she would've been if she could see her Kate today—a lovely young woman, strong in her determination to improve her circumstances and make her world a happier place than when she arrived.

"Oh, quit blathering, you idiot!" Kate said to no one in particular as she sat up to turn on the lamp stationed on the end table next to her bed. Eyeing the book Cecily had loaned her, Kate grabbed for it as she blew her nose into the handkerchief Marcel had offered her earlier that evening.

Honk! Ah-choo! Hiccup!

Kate picked up the book and shuffled the worn pages between her fingers.

"It's certainly not a very lengthy book, but it smells like a book should—ready to be devoured, probably in a single reading."

Kate was tired but not particularly sleepy. And the more she read, the less tired she became.

She had barely started in on the third chapter—Oh, she's no fool. She adores problems…. Any kind of problem…. All grist to my Aunt Jane's mill. So, if you've any problem in your life, put it to her…. She'll tell you the answer.

—when she felt her head nod and the book slip from her fingers. Already half-asleep Kate lowered her head onto the soft down pillow and would've fallen the rest of the way into her usual comatose state of slumber had her bed not started to move. First it jiggled, then vibrated, then pitched to the left and to the right, finally turning in what felt like 360° circles.

"What in the . . . ?" She heard herself babble as she hung onto the sheets for dear life.

Startled but nonetheless curious, Kate's mind began to rifle through all the obvious possibilities.

Sick to my stomach? No! Having a nightmare? No! Definitely not! This after all was kind of fun!! Well then, what the blood hell was going on?

Then it hit her. "Earthquake!" She yelled as she abruptly sat up in bed. She knew she had very little time to get to a place of safety, but where exactly could that be? *Ah, yes! The bathtub!*

No sooner had she placed her feet on the floor, however, than a ceiling tile overhead, pointed end first, came crashing down, hitting her point blank on the left side of her forehead and scalp, knocking her completely out!

Her final thought?

I wonder how Miss Marple would've dealt with this?

Continue unraveling the adventures of Millicent Winthrop…

About the Author
Gwen Overland

Born and raised near the Puget Sound in Washington State, Gwen and her family now live in Ashland, Oregon, home of the Oregon Shakespeare Festival. Prior to that Gwen lived in Los Angeles and had careers in directing, acting, and singing while performing at the piano. After years in academia, writing one research article followed by another, Gwen turned her talents toward writing fiction and found she happily could not stop.

In addition to writing romance, she also writes chic lit and cozy mysteries under the pseudonym, Gwen Overland writing as Cunigunda Valentine (believe it or not, her grandmother's name).

When she's not reading, writing, or playing with her two black pugs, Buster Keaton and Emmett Kelly, Gwen works in the theatre, teaches college students how to muster the courage to follow their dreams, or assists psychotherapy clients in discovering more joy and meaning in their lives.

Keep up with Gwen by following her on Twitter @gwenoverland; Gwen Overland Author on Facebook; @GwenOverland on Instagram, or at www.gwenoverland.com and www.cunigundavalentine.com.

Thank you so much for purchasing this book from the Millicent Winthrop series.

The Greatest Compliment a Writer Can Receive Is a Written Review from a Reader!

If you enjoyed reading this book, please take the time to write a review to post on Amazon, Barnes and Noble, or wherever else you purchased the book. It doesn't matter if it's long or short, stellar or less than positive; a review is one of the best ways to let others know how you responded to this author's work.

Gwen Overland as Cunigunda Valentine

Made in the USA
San Bernardino, CA
15 February 2019